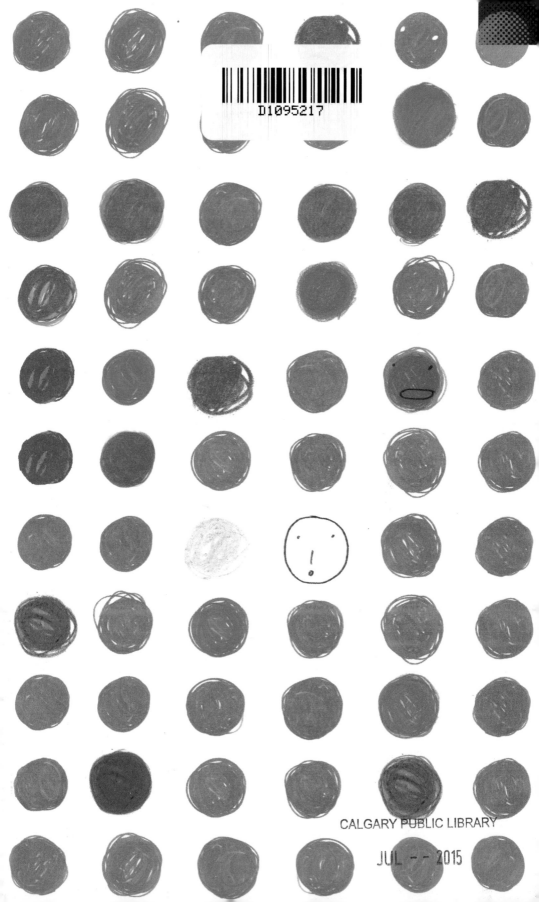

D1095217

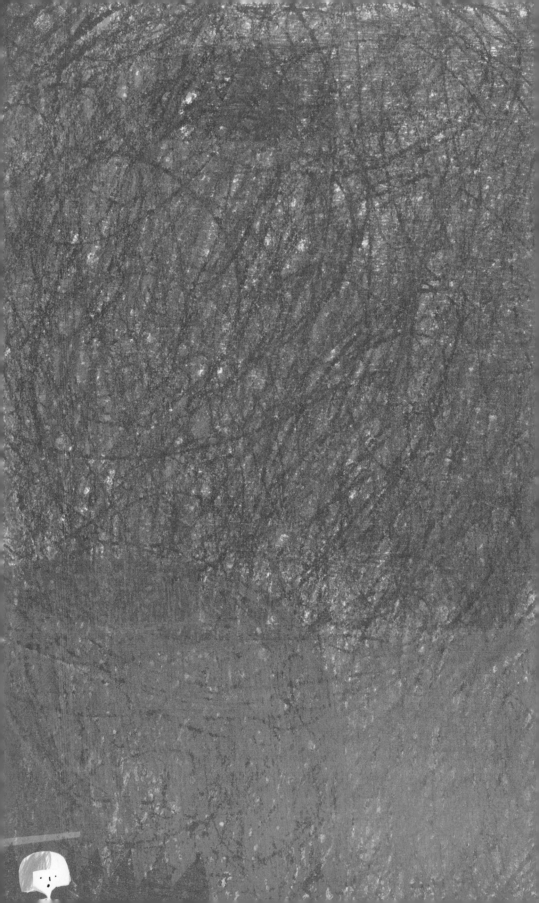

THERE'S SOME SORT OF BEAST LIVING IN MY BELLY...

GRZEGORZ
KASDEPKE

THE BEAST
IN MY
BELLY

ILLUSTRATED BY TOMEK KOZŁOWSKI
TRANSLATED BY AGNES MONOD-GAYRAUD

ENCHANTED LION BOOKS
NEW YORK

1.

"There's a beast in my belly," I announced. "Just listen!"

Dad put his ear against my belly, but the sneaky beast went completely silent.

"I can't hear a thing," Dad said.

"Maybe you frightened it," I whispered.

"Maybe," Dad said, nodding his head in concern.

I turned to Mom to tell her about the beast.

"There's a beast in my belly," I said.

"Oh?" said Mom, looking up from her book. "Is it serious?"

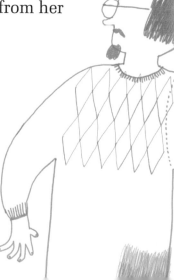

"I think it might be quite serious," I replied. "The beast is growling."

But when Mom put her ear against my belly, the beast didn't let out a single squeak.

So I went to tell my brother about it.

"There's a beast in my belly."

"Sure there is," he said, laughing at me.

"It must be the chicken you ate for lunch."

That's how families can be. Sometimes they just don't take you seriously.

2.

As soon as we were on our own again, the beast began to purr softly. I played with my dolls and did my best to ignore it, but the purr only got louder and louder.

"So now you decide to speak up," I said grumpily. "Before you were as quiet as a mouse." At the mention of a mouse, the beast began to liven up even more.

So maybe this beast was actually a cat. Had I accidentally swallowed a cat and now this cat felt like swallowing a mouse?

"Are you a cat?" I asked the beast.

It growled in reply.

So maybe the beast was really a dog. Had I swallowed a dog and now this dog wanted to chase a cat?

"Are you a dog?" I asked the beast.

It let out a ferocious roar.

Could it be a lion? Had I swallowed a lion that wanted to get its paws on a dog?

"Are you a lion?" I asked the beast, but the beast grew quiet and didn't make another sound. Not a peep, even though I rubbed my belly right up until dinnertime.

So maybe the beast wasn't a lion after all. Maybe it was the sort of beast that was afraid of lions. Besides, who ever heard of a girl swallowing a lion? It was usually the other way around!

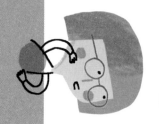

3.

"There's a beast in my belly," I said to Grandma the next day.

"Impossible!" she said, cutting the cheesecake into slices.

"It's *very* possible," I said. "Just listen!"

But once again the beast went quiet, so I went to tell Grandpa about it.

"There's a beast in my belly," I told him.

"What's this?" Grandpa asked, looking up from his newspaper.

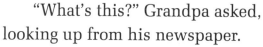

"Really! You have to listen."

But the stubborn beast didn't make another peep.

I was so upset I didn't want my slice of cake. I walked home feeling miserable, while the beast made whimpering sounds like it was sorry. Maybe it was as upset as I was. Maybe it had been hoping for some tasty cake too.

4.

In the afternoon, the beast and I went for a walk in the park. We watched all the people passing by.

"Would you like to have a dog of your own?" a man in glasses asked as we went up to his puppy.

"I may already have one," I replied.

"Really?" said the man.

"There's a beast in my belly," I explained. "I think it could be a dog."

The man smiled, shook his head, and went on his way.

"Would you like to have a cat of
your own?" asked a lady in a long coat
when she noticed me peeking at her cat
in its carrier.

"I may already have one," I told her.

"Is that so?" she said, surprised.

"There's a beast in my belly," I
explained. "I think it could be a cat."

The lady chuckled and went on
her way.

The beast and I sat down on a bench
next to some squirrels and birds and a
pond full of carp.

The beast hadn't wanted to play with
any of the other animals, but it rumbled at
the sight of the carp. Maybe the beast was
actually a fish?

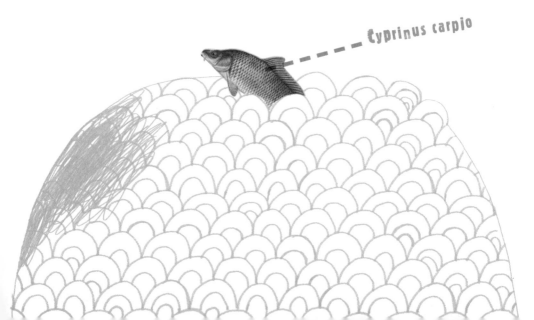

Cyprinus carpio

5.

When I got home, my aunt was there.

"There's a beast in my belly!" I called to her from the front door.

"You don't say!" she called back, sounding amused.

So I went to tell my uncle about it.

"There's a beast in my belly."

"How do you like that!" my uncle said with a big grin.

No one believed me. Not a single one.

I made a mad face and marched off to my room. That was it! I wouldn't be having my snack with them.

The beast growled grumpily, like it knew it wouldn't be having anything at snack time either.

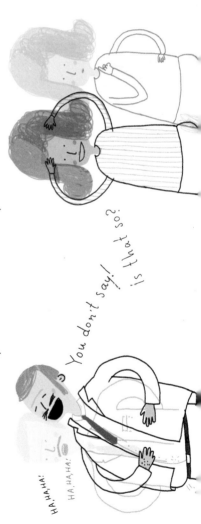

6.

After dinner, the beast stopped making any noise at all.

"Are you still there?" I asked as I splashed around in the bath.

The beast didn't make a sound.

"Hello?" I shouted.

The beast stayed quiet.

"Are you asleep?" I whispered.

Nothing. Not a peep.

What if something had happened to the beast?

What if it didn't like taking baths?

I jumped out of the tub, straight into my pajamas.

The beast purred happily, so I guess it wasn't a fish after all.

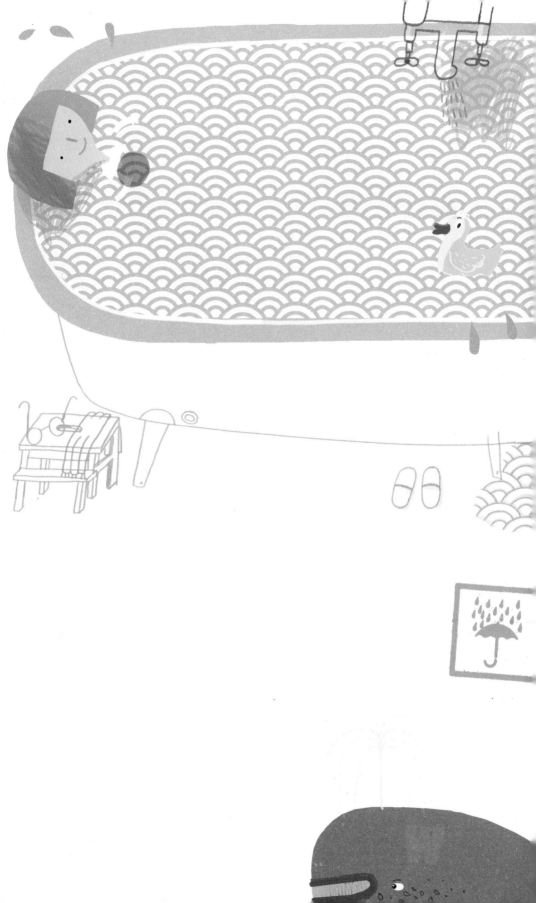

7.

"Some beasts sleep at night and others
sleep during the day," Dad explained as he
tucked me into bed.

"What about mine?" I wanted to know.

"Yours?" he asked, confused.

"The beast in my belly, remember? Do
you think it sleeps at night or during the
day?"

"Ah, yes, the beast in your belly," Dad
said. "I suspect it's the sort that sleeps at
night."

Then he gave me a kiss and turned off
the light, leaving me alone with the beast.

We lay there in the dark.

"Are you afraid?" I whispered.

The beast let out a soft bark.

"So am I," I told it. "But only a little."

Just in case, I turned the lamp back on.

"If any ghosts appear, just growl at them, okay?"

The beast rumbled in agreement.

"Goodnight," I said, stretching from the tips of my fingers to the tips of my toes.

"Goodnight," the beast gurgled back.

8.

It turned out that my kind of beast only sleeps through half the night.

He woke me up when everyone else was still snoring away in bed.

He led me into the kitchen, right up to the refrigerator. When I opened it, I discovered what a greedy beast it was! It wouldn't go back to sleep until it had eaten not one, not two, not three, but *four* sausages!

9.

At breakfast the next morning, I looked at my belly and said, "Let's see what else you like to eat."

"What's that?" asked Mom.

"I'm talking to my beast," I replied.

"What beast?"

"The beast in my belly," I reminded her. "I've already told you about it!"

She shrugged and my brother rolled his eyes. I ignored them both.

"Let's see if you like these rolls," I said, reaching into the bread basket.

The beast liked them very much.

"How about some cheese?" I asked.

It liked the cheese too.

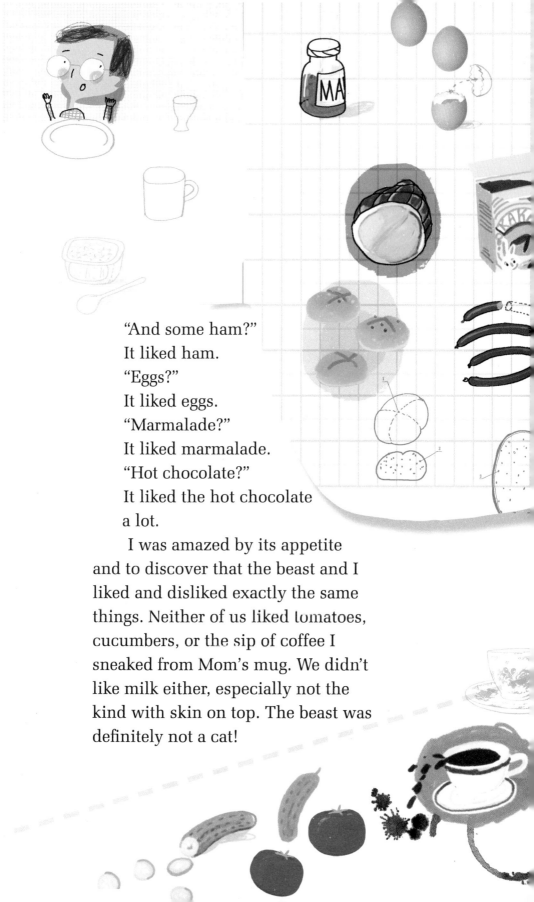

"And some ham?"
It liked ham.
"Eggs?"
It liked eggs.
"Marmalade?"
It liked marmalade.
"Hot chocolate?"
It liked the hot chocolate
a lot.

I was amazed by its appetite
and to discover that the beast and I
liked and disliked exactly the same
things. Neither of us liked tomatoes,
cucumbers, or the sip of coffee I
sneaked from Mom's mug. We didn't
like milk either, especially not the
kind with skin on top. The beast was
definitely not a cat!

10.

"There's a beast in my belly!" I announced to everyone at preschool.

"No there's not!" shouted the girls, probably because they were jealous.

"It's true!" I shouted back.

I went to tell the boys, but they didn't believe me either.

"I do too!" I told them.

Then I went to find the teacher.

"There's a beast in my belly," I told her.

"Are you sure?" she said, smiling. "Be careful it doesn't eat you up!"

I smiled too, but later I began to worry. Maybe my beast was actually a crocodile?

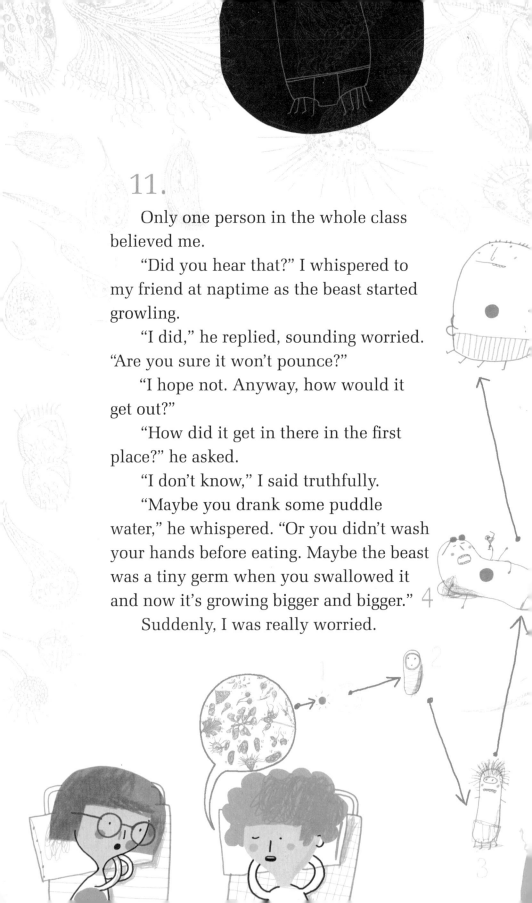

11.

Only one person in the whole class believed me.

"Did you hear that?" I whispered to my friend at naptime as the beast started growling.

"I did," he replied, sounding worried. "Are you sure it won't pounce?"

"I hope not. Anyway, how would it get out?"

"How did it get in there in the first place?" he asked.

"I don't know," I said truthfully.

"Maybe you drank some puddle water," he whispered. "Or you didn't wash your hands before eating. Maybe the beast was a tiny germ when you swallowed it and now it's growing bigger and bigger."

Suddenly, I was really worried.

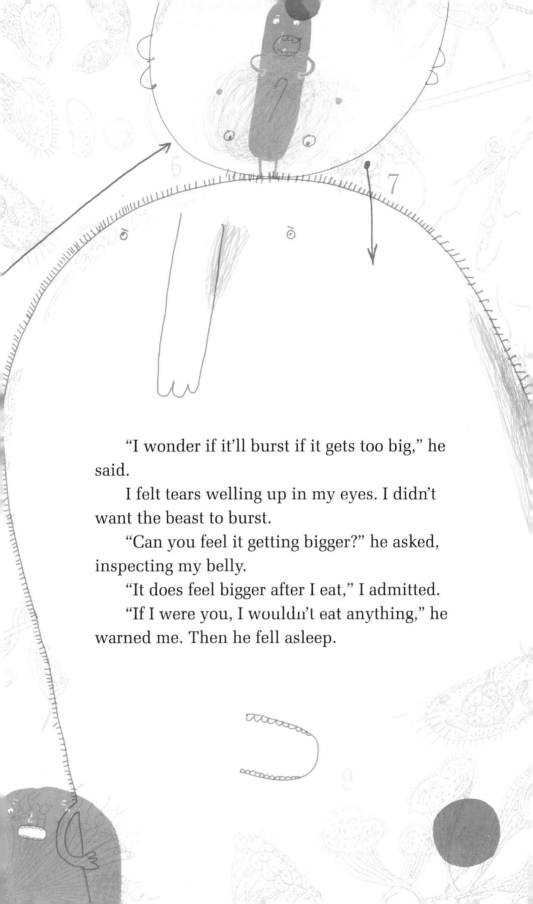

"I wonder if it'll burst if it gets too big," he said.

I felt tears welling up in my eyes. I didn't want the beast to burst.

"Can you feel it getting bigger?" he asked, inspecting my belly.

"It does feel bigger after I eat," I admitted.

"If I were you, I wouldn't eat anything," he warned me. Then he fell asleep.

12.

I didn't have any lunch. Not one sip of soup or a bite of dessert. Boy, did that make the beast mad! It roared and rumbled, it whined and groaned. Finally, it began to growl in a sad sort of way.

Some of the boys and girls pressed their ears against my belly. Others ran away like they were really scared. Our teacher wasn't happy about all of the commotion.

"What's going on here?" she asked in a stern voice.

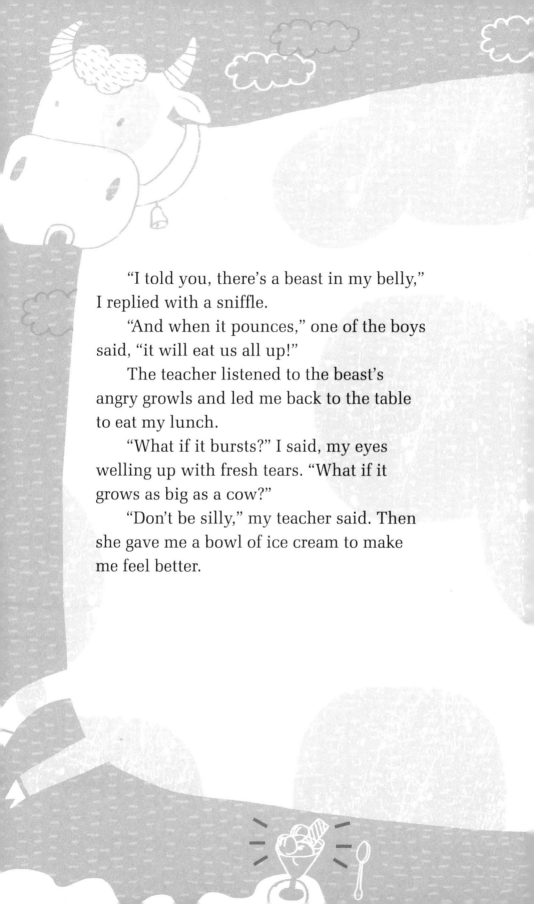

"I told you, there's a beast in my belly," I replied with a sniffle.

"And when it pounces," one of the boys said, "it will eat us all up!"

The teacher listened to the beast's angry growls and led me back to the table to eat my lunch.

"What if it bursts?" I said, my eyes welling up with fresh tears. "What if it grows as big as a cow?"

"Don't be silly," my teacher said. Then she gave me a bowl of ice cream to make me feel better.

13.

After that, a strange thing happened. The beast stopped growling for good. I listened and listened and listened, and so did everyone else, but we didn't hear a single groan or growl. Nothing.

I patted my belly.

Still nothing.

Had the beast escaped without anyone noticing?

We looked around feeling really worried. It could be hiding anywhere!

14.

Suddenly, we heard a gurgle of steam across the room and someone whispered, "It's in the radiator!"

Then some girls heard the water gurgling in the pipes and squealed, "It's in the bathroom!"

We pricked up our ears, but the beast was so speedy it was hard to tell exactly where it was. After the sink pipes, it sounded like it leapt onto the squeaking hinge of the door and out into the street. There it roared and sputtered from the engine of a car like an enormous beast. It didn't sound like a harmless little creature anymore at all!

And to think that just this morning it had been living in my belly!

15.

Once the beast was gone, I began to worry about it. What if it needed help? Where would it live? Who would feed it?

I looked for the beast the whole way home but didn't see it anywhere.

"It will manage on its own," Mom assured me.

"What if it doesn't?" I moaned.

"Someone will take it in," Dad said.

They were trying to comfort me, but it felt like they really didn't care at all.

So it was a big surprise when my brother came into my room before dinner and said, "Listen to this!"

I put my ear against his belly and jumped straight up to the ceiling. Something was growling in there!

"Now your beast is in my belly," he said with a grin.

"Will you take care of it?" I asked.

"I will," he promised. "In fact, I'm going to feed it right now."

We went to the dinner table together. I wanted to make sure my brother fed the beast properly. It must have grown a lot since it left my belly, because it ate a ton. And it turned out that it liked tomatoes after all.

I felt a little jealous of my brother, but after dinner he helped me put up a sign that said:

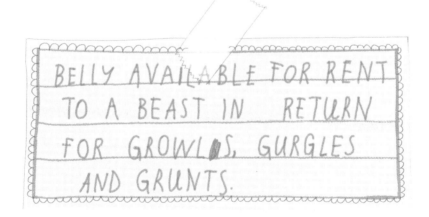

BELLY AVAILABLE FOR RENT
TO A BEAST IN RETURN
FOR GROWLS, GURGLES
AND GRUNTS.

With thanks to Mercedes Pritchett for her
wonderful work on the translation. — ELB

www.enchantedlionbooks.com

First published in 2015 by Enchanted Lion Books,
351 Van Brunt Street, Brooklyn, NY 11231

Originally published in 2012 by Wydawnictwo Dwie Siostry, Warsaw, Poland, as
W Moim Bruzuchu Mieszka Jakies Zwierzatko.

Printed by South China Printing Company
First Printing